THE LEGEND OF ROCK PAPER SCISSORS

DREW DAYWALT

ADAM REX

HarperCollins *Children's Books*

1… 2… 3…

To my champions,
Roger Di Paolo
Tom Stephan
Rose Mary Piazza Stehman-Humble

— D.D.

For Henry

— A.R.

GO!

HarperCollins Publishers
Since 1817

First published in hardback in the USA by Balzer and Bray,
an imprint of HarperCollins *Publishers*, in 2017

First published in hardback in Great Britain by HarperCollins *Children's Books* in 2017

1 3 5 7 9 10 8 6 4 2

ISBN: 978-0-00-825239-7

HarperCollins *Children's Books* is a division of HarperCollins *Publishers* Ltd.

Typography by Adam Rex and Dana Fritts

A CIP catalogue record for this book is available from the British Library.

Visit our website at: www.harpercollins.co.uk

Printed and bound in China

Long ago,

in an ancient and distant realm called
the Kingdom of Backgarden,

there lived a warrior named

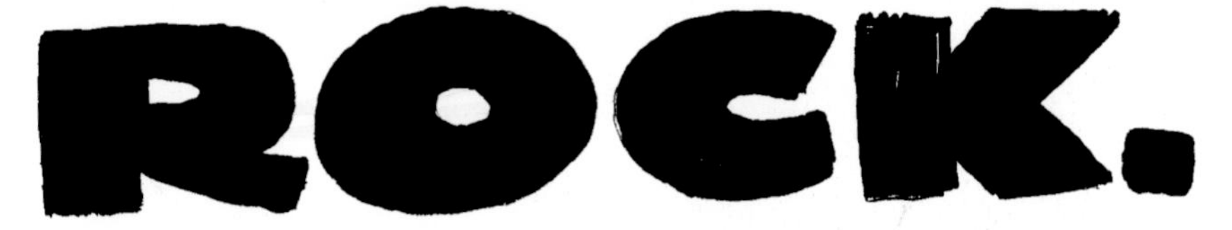

Rock was the strongest in
all the land, but he was
sad because no one could
give him a worthy challenge.

Rock travelled to
the mysterious Forest
of Over by the Tyre Swing,
where he met a warrior
who hung on a rope,
holding a giant's underwear.

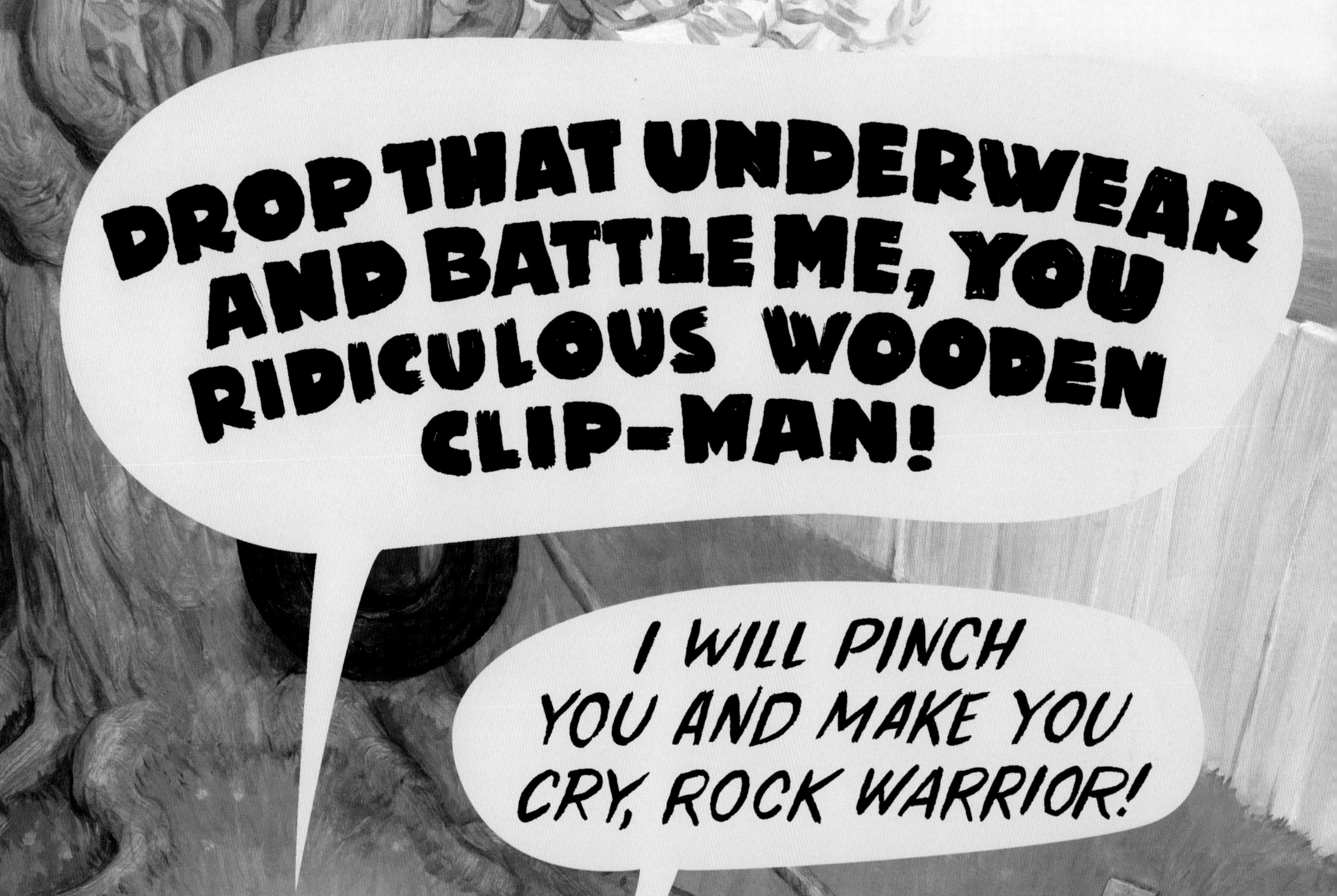
DROP THAT UNDERWEAR AND BATTLE ME, YOU RIDICULOUS WOODEN CLIP-MAN!
I WILL PINCH YOU AND MAKE YOU CRY, ROCK WARRIOR!

ROCK
VERSUS
CLOTHESPEG!

HENRY
ROCK IS
VICTORIOUS!

Even though he had won, Rock was still unsatisfied.

So he journeyed on, to the mystical Tower of Grandma's Favourite Apricot Tree.

There he was met by an odd and delicious fruit.

YOU, SIR, LOOK LIKE A FUZZY LITTLE BUM.
WHAT?!
I challenge you to a duel!
THEN LET US BATTLE!

ROCK VERSUS APRICOT!

I will beat you, Rock, with my tart and tangy sweetness!

ROCK IS VICTORIOUS!

ARE YOU NOT ENTERTAINED?!

They *were* entertained.

But the battle had been too easy. So Rock left the Kingdom of Backgarden, still in search of a worthy foe.

Meanwhile,

in the Empire of Mum's Study,

on lonely and windswept Desk Mountain, a second great warrior sought the glory of battle.

And his name was Paper.

Even though he was the cleverest warrior in all the land, he was also sad, because no one could outwit him.

He set out across Desk Mountain to find his match. There he met a large and square monster.

Paper versus Computer Printer!

NOOOO!
NOT A PAPER JAM!
{:0
PAPER IS VICTORIOUS!

Having beaten the fiercest fighter of Desk Mountain, Paper climbed down to the Pit of Office Rubbish Bin, where he battled the most terrifying horde of creatures in all the land . . .

the HALF-EATEN BAG OF TRAIL MIX!

PAPER
VERSUS
HALF-EATEN
BAG OF
TRAIL
MIX!

AHHHHH! Foul wizard! He's blotted out the sun!
Run for your lives, laddies!

PAPER WINS AGAIN!

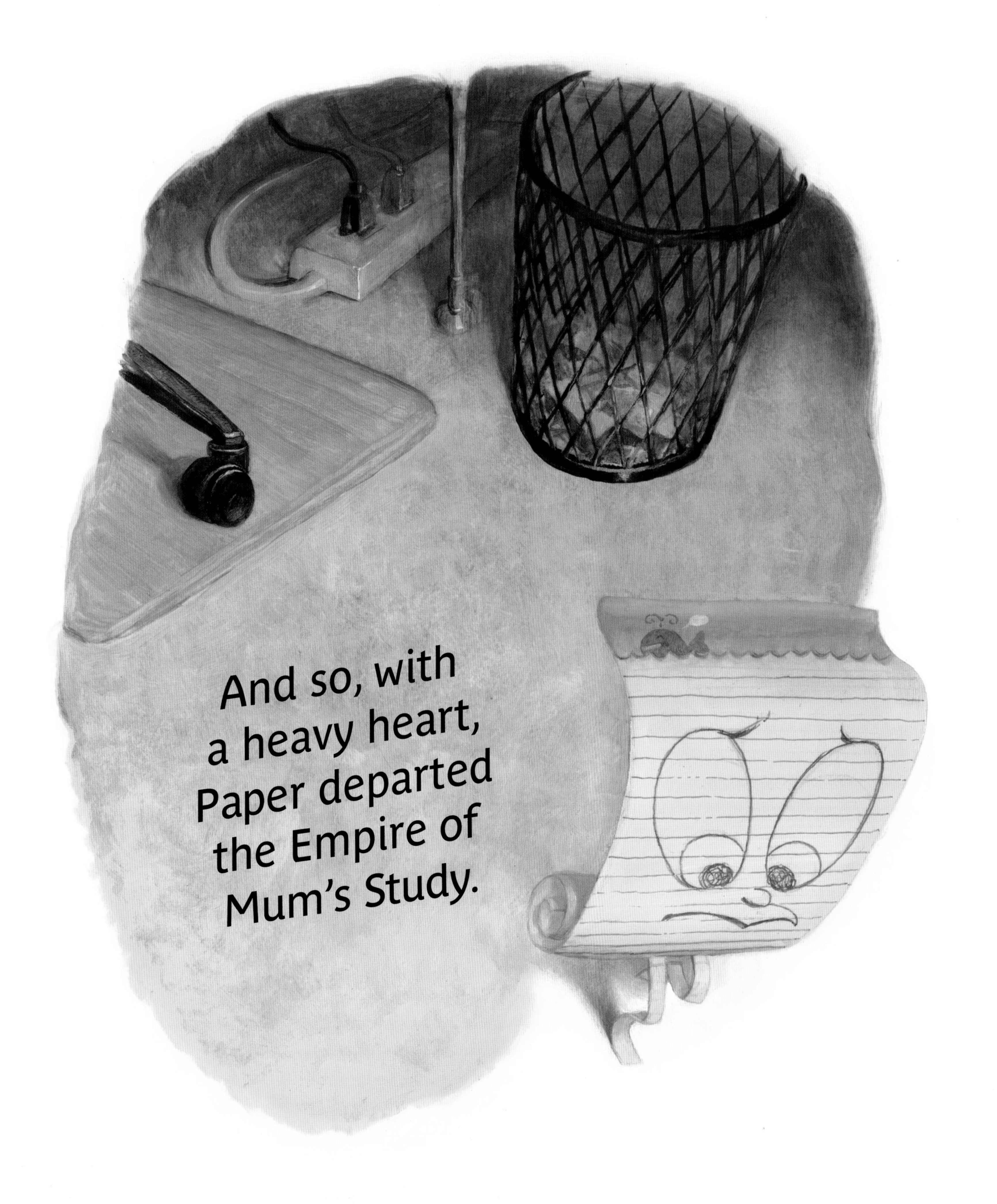

And so, with
a heavy heart,
Paper departed
the Empire of
Mum's Study.

At the same time,

in the Kitchen Realm,

in the tiny village of Junk Drawer,
there lived a third great warrior.

They called her Scissors,

and she was the fastest blade in
all the land. She, too, was unchallenged.
On this day, her first opponent was a
strange and sticky circle-man.

Let us do battle, you tacky and vaguely round monstrosity!
I will battle you, and I will leave you beaten and confused with my adhesive and tangling powers!
IMPROVED

SCISSORS IS VICTORIOUS!

Scissors forged on across the Kitchen Realm
to the frigid wastes of Refrigerator/Freezer.
There she met her most fearsome adversaries yet . . .
dinosaurs made of frozen breaded chicken.

Cheese CHUM
I have come from the far reaches of Kitchen to battle you, O bizarre and yummy breaded dinosaurs!
Bow before our child-pleasing shapes and flavours, sword master!
No one can resist our crunchy awesomeness!

SCISSORS VERSUS
DINOSAUR-
CHICKEN
SHAPED
NUGGETS!
DINOSAUR-
SHAPED CHICKEN
NUGGETS WIN...?

No, wait!
No, No, they don't!
SCISSORS IS VICTORIOUS AGAIN!

AM I SO GOOD THAT NOT EVEN DINOSAUR-SHAPED CHICKEN NUGGETS CAN BEAT ME?

And so Scissors,
like Rock and Paper
before her, travelled beyond her
own kingdom, seeking out a
challenger who was her equal.

Then one day,
in the great cavern
of Two-Car Garage,

Rock and Scissors
came face-to-face.

I hope you're wearing your battle pants, rock warrior.
IF BY "BATTLE PANTS" YOU MEAN "NO PANTS, BUT I'M WILLING TO FIGHT YOU," THEN YES . . . YES, I AM WEARING MY BATTLE PANTS, WEIRD SCISSORY ONE!

VERSUS

ISSORS

An epic
and legendary battle
ensued, but ultimately . . .

IS VICTORIOUS!

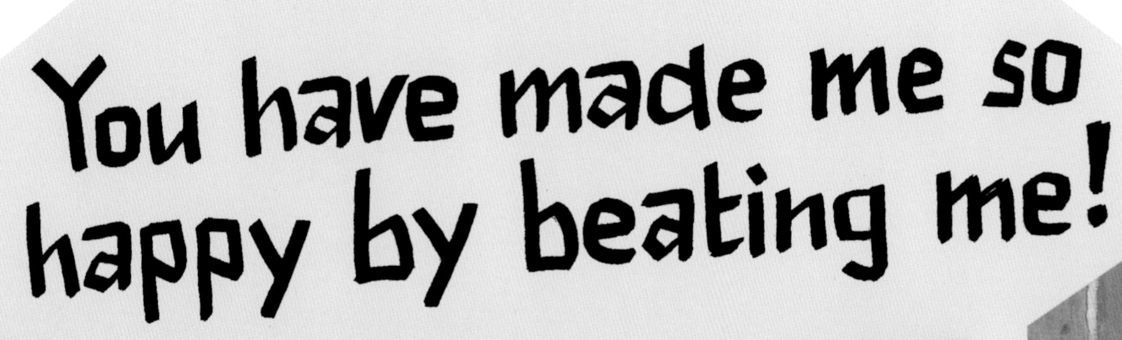
You have made me so happy by beating me!

I WISH I FELT YOUR JOY, SCISSORS, FOR I HAVE YET TO MEET A WARRIOR WHO CAN BEAT ME.

Hi there.

THOSE ARE FIGHTING WORDS!

Wait. What?

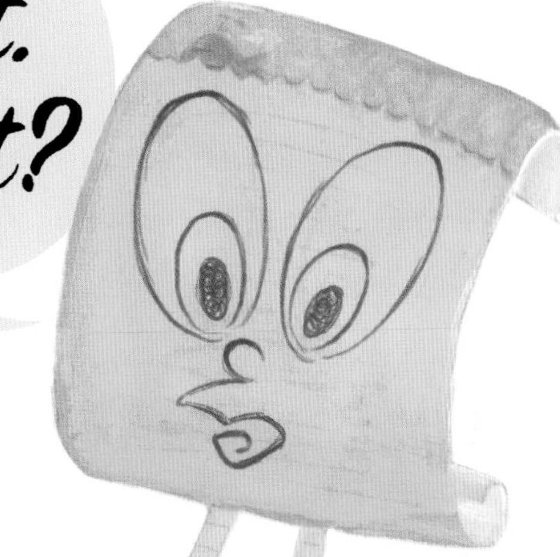

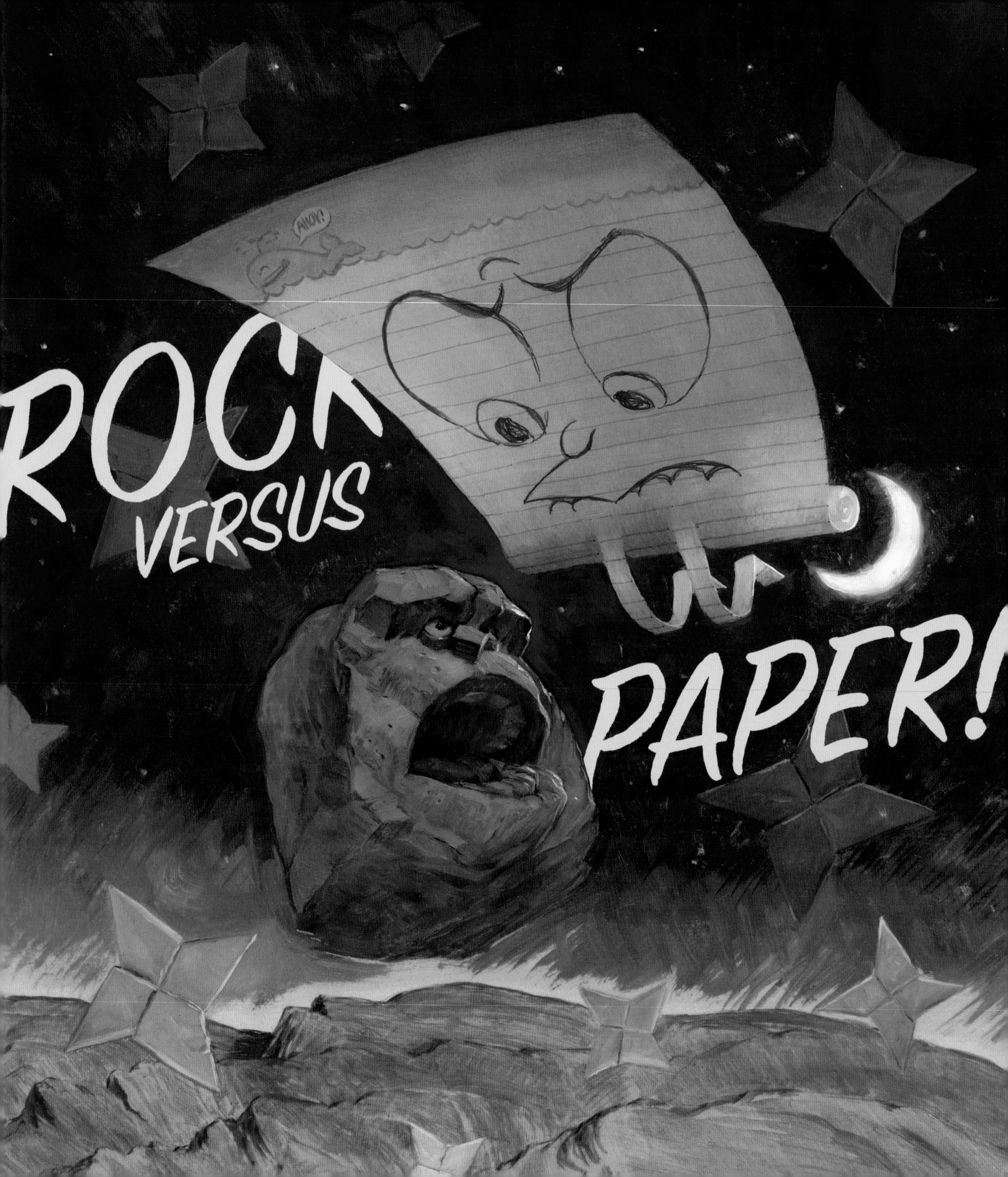

ROCK
VERSUS
PAPER!

THIS IS THE BEST DAY OF MY LIFE! THANK YOU FOR WINNING, O GREAT KNIGHT OF PAPER!
That's fine for you, but it looks as though no one will ever beat me.

Not so fast,
Paper!
Wait.
What?

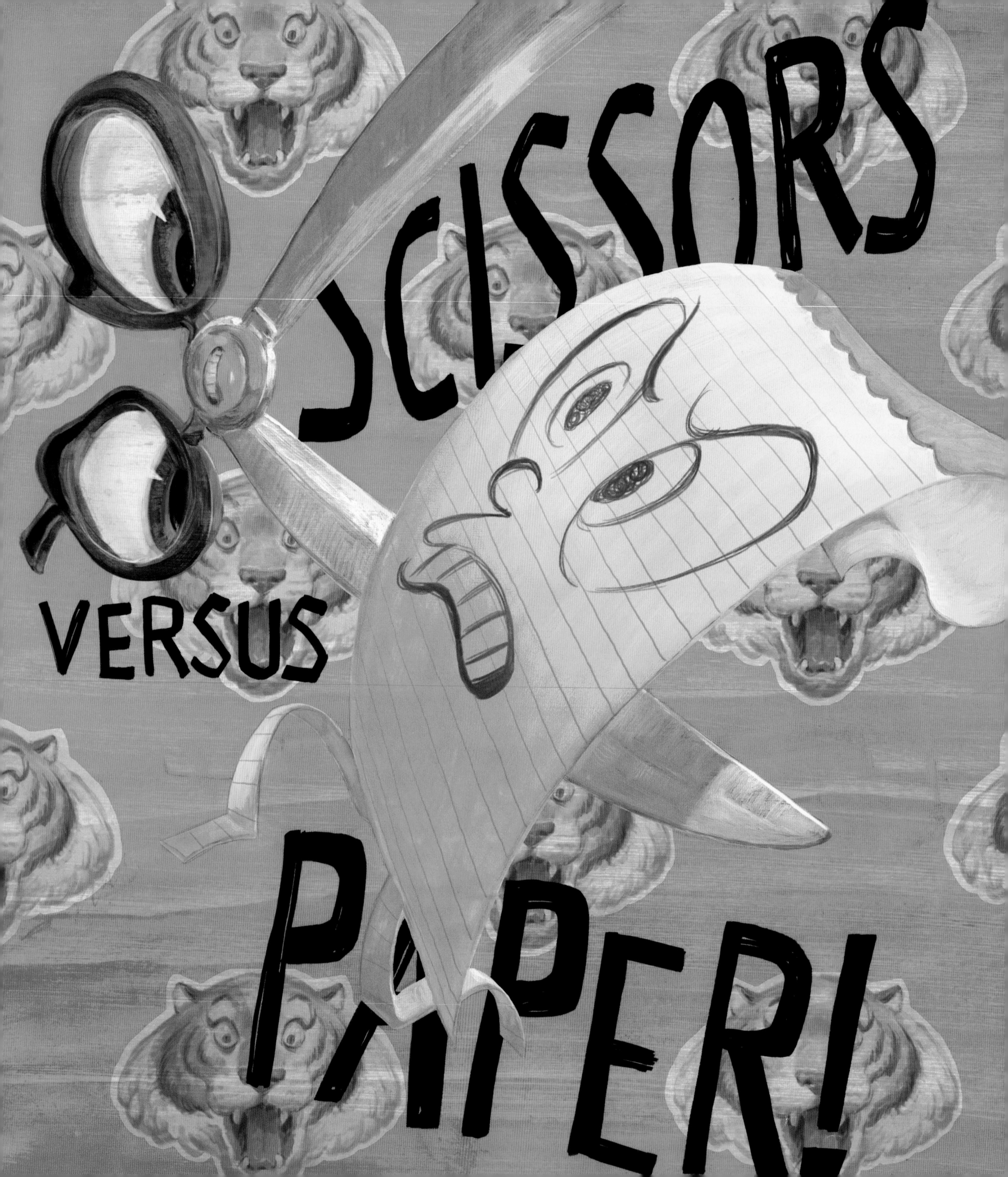
SCISSORS
VERSUS
PAPER!

You beat me!

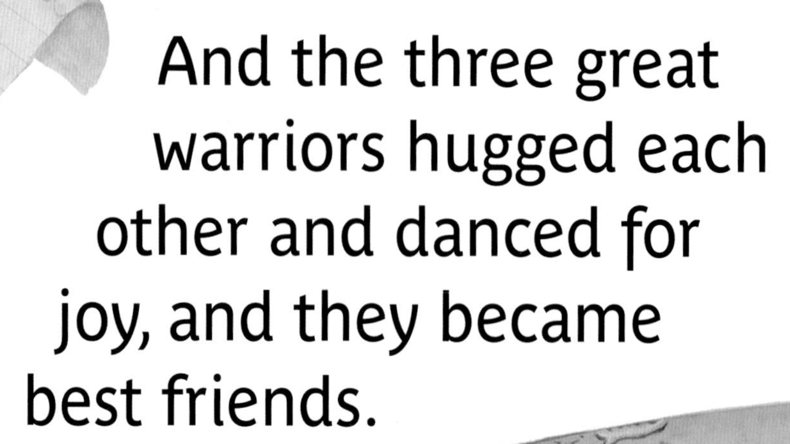

And the three great warriors hugged each other and danced for joy, and they became best friends.

Finally, they had each met their matches. They were so happy, in fact, that they began to battle again.

Round and round they went, in the most massive and epic three-way battle of all time! And it is said that this joyous struggle still rages on to this very day.

That is why children around the world – in back gardens, on playgrounds, and yes, even in classrooms – still honour the three great warriors by playing . . .

ROCK,
PAPER,
SCISSORS!